I SURVIVED

THE CALIFORNIA WILDFIRES, 2018

by Lauren Tarshis

illustrated by Scott Dawson

Scholastic Inc.

Text copyright © 2020 by Dreyfuss Tarshis Media Inc.
Illustrations copyright © 2020 by Scholastic Inc.
Photos ©: 119: Courtesy of the Fisher Family; 121, 122: Courtesy of the author; 126: John G Mabanglo/EPA-EFE/Shutterstock; 128: Archives & Special Collections, Mansfield Library, University of Montana; 129: Jim Zuckerman/Getty Images; 130: Mark Ralston/AFP/Getty Images; 132: USGS/Alamy Stock Photo; 133: Fred Greaves/Reuters/Newscom; 134: Michael Routh/Ambient Images/Newscom; 135: Boise Mobile Equipment 2018; 136: Kari Greer/US Forest Service; 137: Signal Photos/Alamy Stock Photo.
Special thanks to Ron Steffens

This book is being published simultaneously in hardcover by Scholastic Press.

All rights reserved. Published by Scholastic Inc., *Publishers since 1920*. SCHOLASTIC, SCHOLASTIC PRESS, and associated logos are trademarks and/or registered trademarks of Scholastic Inc.

The publisher does not have any control over and does not assume any responsibility for author or third-party websites or their content.

While inspired by real events and historical characters, this is a work of fiction and does not claim to be historically accurate or to portray factual events or relationships. Please keep in mind that references to actual persons, living or dead, business establishments, events, or locales may not be factually accurate, but rather fictionalized by the author.

ISBN 978-1-338-31744-2

10 9 8 7 6 5 4 3 2   20 21 22 23 24

Printed in the U.S.A.   40
First printing 2020
Designed by Katie Fitch

To
Holly, Josh, Lucas, and Sienna Fisher
and
Nicole, Greg, and Eleanor Weddig

CHAPTER 1

Josh stared in horror at the bloodred glow rising up behind him. A massive wildfire was raging through the forest, a wall of flames devouring everything in its path. Josh and his cousin Holly were in a race for their lives.

"Josh!" Holly shouted, grabbing his hand. "This way!"

As they took off along the forest path, the hot

1

wind gusted hard. Suddenly the air was filled with sparks and glowing embers and chunks of flaming wood. Josh felt them landing on his bare arms and legs, sizzling against his skin, searing his scalp. He tried to brush them away. But they were all over him, biting into his skin like the white-hot teeth of a flesh-eating monster.

He and Holly ran faster, but the wall of flames was closing in from behind. And all around them, the burning embers were setting fires wherever they landed.

On treetops.

WHOOSH!

On branches.

WHOOSH!

On the forest floor.

WHOOSH! WHOOSH! WHOOSH!

With every gust of wind, more embers swirled. Flames shot higher and higher into the sky. A nightmare of sounds crashed against Josh's ears. The fire's roar, the moaning wind, the cracking and snapping of the trees. It was as though the air itself was shrieking in agony.

Josh glanced around, struggling to breathe in the thickening smoke. Just minutes before, the forest had been peaceful and green. Now it was a terrifying maze of fire.

How could everything change so fast?

And then:

Boom!

A burning pine tree in front of them exploded. Shards of splintered wood sprayed out. Holly tried to pull Josh sideways, but Josh stumbled. When he looked up, there was a flaming branch speeding through the air.

It was headed straight for his skull.

CHAPTER 2

Josh snatched the basketball from the air and sprinted down the court. They were down by two points, just seconds left in the game. A monster of a kid was all over Josh, trying to steal the ball. But Josh spun around and took the shot just as the buzzer blared.

Swish!

4

Three points! They'd won!

Josh dropped to his knees in happy shock. His team swarmed around him, smothering him in sweaty hugs.

"You were unstoppable!" said Josh's best friend, Greg, as they trotted off the court. "That shot was *sick*!"

"You played great, too," Josh said, putting an arm around Greg's skinny shoulders.

Josh glanced up into the stands, wishing his father had been there to see his buzzer beater. Dad was going to *freak* when he found out that Josh had made a three-pointer!

Josh had been practicing in the driveway for months, shooting and missing, shooting and missing, with Dad always cheering him on. "Don't give up!" he'd shout. Dad always told Josh he could do anything he set his mind to.

"Just look at *me*," he'd say.

Dad had grown up with practically nothing. He'd worked his butt off. Now he was one of the top guys at the big New York City bank where he worked. Everyone loved Tim Wallace. And

Josh admired his father more than anyone in the world.

Josh packed up his stuff and said goodbye to his coach.

"Need a ride?" Greg asked as they headed out into the parking lot.

"I'm good," Josh said, high-fiving Greg. "I'm sure my mom is on her way."

But five minutes passed, then ten. All Josh's friends had left, and Mom still wasn't there. She hadn't been feeling great today; that's why she'd skipped the game. But Josh could swear she'd said she'd be here to pick him up.

Josh texted her, but she didn't answer.

He was about to call Dad, but changed his mind. Dad was working at home today and was stressed out by an important deal he was working on. Josh knew he shouldn't bug him.

Why not walk home? Josh thought. His house was maybe a mile away. The walk wouldn't kill him. He texted Mom his plan, slung his drawstring bag over his shoulders, and headed out of the parking lot. He walked along the sidewalk of the busy road, trying to stay in the shade.

It was crazy hot — nobody could remember such a broiling summer. Josh kicked a stone along the sidewalk, imagining a cool ocean wave crashing over him and washing his sweat away. That's where he should be right now, actually, splashing around in the ocean at the Jersey Shore. Usually, in July, Mom and Dad and Josh spent two weeks there, in a hotel right on the beach.

But a couple of weeks ago, Mom and Dad broke the news: They had to cancel the trip.

"Sorry, buddy," Dad had said. "Too much happening at work right now."

Josh was pretty bummed. He kicked the rock again, thinking about the pool at the hotel. It had a waterslide and a high diving board.

But he understood why they couldn't go. You didn't become a superstar like Dad by blowing off work to lie around on the beach. At least they had their pool at home. It didn't have a waterslide, but it was still pretty sweet.

Josh reached his neighborhood, where the big houses were mostly hidden behind fences and stone walls. He smiled to himself as he imagined what Dad would say when Josh told him about his winning basket.

"You're a champ!" he'd boom.

Josh rounded the last corner and then stopped short when his house came into view. His heart started to pound. There were two cars parked in his driveway.

Police cars.

Josh's brain flooded with nightmare scenes: Shattered windows. Pools of blood. Crumpled bodies.

But nothing could have prepared him for what he saw as he sprinted up the driveway. His whole body started to prickle, like tiny alarms were buzzing under his skin. Mom was standing in the doorway, her eyes wide with shock. Two police officers were leading a man to a police car.

The man was in handcuffs.

The man was Dad.

CHAPTER 3

SIX DAYS LATER
TUESDAY, JULY 17, 2018
A WINDING ROAD IN NORTHERN
CALIFORNIA
AROUND 1:15 P.M.

New Jersey Man Arrested

Tim Wallace, 42 years old, of North Creek, New Jersey, was arrested Wednesday afternoon. He is accused of stealing millions of dollars from the bank where he has worked for 15 years.

"Josh," Mom said, looking over from the driver's seat. "Don't read those stories. They're just going to upset you."

"Sorry, Mom," Josh said, letting his phone drop to his lap. Mom was right. These articles about Dad were total garbage, filled with lies.

Of course Dad didn't steal money from the bank! It was all a mix-up, some problem with the bank's computer. Dad said it happened all the time.

The police must have known right away they'd made a mistake; they let Dad come home just a few hours after they arrested him. Now all Dad had to do was go to court and explain everything to a judge. Or something like that. What mattered was that soon this whole mess would be all cleared up.

Mom reached over for Josh's hand, but he slid it away. He loved Mom, of course — she was the best. But he wasn't the touchy type. He glanced at her — her hair wasn't all done up, and she had gray circles under her eyes. Poor Mom looked stressed out.

"Let's take a break from reading those stories," she said. "That's why we came here."

Here was the middle of nowhere, somewhere in California. They'd flown into the Sacramento airport this morning, and they'd been driving for what seemed like forever. They were heading to some little town where Mom's cousins lived.

It had been Mom's idea that she and Josh get away while Dad straightened out the mess at the bank.

"We'll have an adventure together," she'd said.

Josh had figured he and Mom would go to the hotel on the shore, like they'd planned.

But Mom had decided this was the perfect chance to visit their cousins — Holly, who was Josh's age, and her mom, Nicole.

Josh knew Mom and Nicole had been buddies when they were little girls. But those two hadn't seen each other in years. And Josh and his mom had never even met Holly.

Mom had showed Josh Holly's picture. She looked friendly enough. But from what Mom had said, he could just tell that he and Holly were different types. She seemed all into nature and stuff like that. Trees could be cool if you could climb them, and Josh loved animals. He'd just rather play video games than die of boredom on a hike.

And where exactly did these cousins live?

Josh stared out the car window. They seemed to be driving through an endless forest. He gripped his phone tighter. At least he could check the Yankees scores and FaceTime with Greg and Dad whenever he wanted.

Josh leaned his head against the window. He was just dozing off when Mom's voice jolted him back to life.

"Josh!" Mom said. "Look at this!"

Josh turned to the window, and his eyes bugged out. They were still driving through the forest. Except every single tree was dead — bare and black and twisted. It looked like an evil witch had cast a killing spell, destroying everything for miles around.

A chill ran down Josh's spine.

What could have happened here?

CHAPTER 4

"Must have been a wildfire," Mom said. "California's had some big ones lately."

They drove more slowly, and Josh took it all in. He'd seen some videos of wildfires — flames shooting up into the sky, black smoke, big planes dumping water and that bright red foam from the sky.

But none of it seemed real. It was like a clip from a disaster movie, or even a video game. Josh hadn't thought about what it really meant for a whole forest to burn up.

Now Josh gaped at the dead trees around

him — there had to be thousands of them. They reminded him of skeletons, all bare and charred and twisted, their spiked branches reaching out like bony arms. He was glad when he and Mom finally drove out of the burned area, and the forest turned green again.

A little ways up, Mom stopped at a small store so they could get some snacks.

"Looks like you had a fire around here," Mom said to the gray-haired woman at the cash register.

"Sure did," the woman said, ringing up their chips and waters. "July of 2015. Burned for a whole week."

"Goodness!" Mom said.

"Lost some houses, too," the woman added, shaking her head sadly. "These fires are happening more and more. Up and down California. Other places, too."

"Why is that?" Mom asked, swiping her credit card.

"I'm no scientist," the woman said, putting their snacks into a paper bag. "But it has to be the weather — everything's out of whack. Our summers are so long and hot; we hardly get any rain anymore."

"Our weather's strange in New Jersey, too," Mom said.

That's for sure, Josh thought.

And not just the broiling summers. Winters were wild, too. One day you could get frostbite from the cold and the next day it was warm enough to wear a T-shirt.

Mom wished the woman luck and they left the store. Josh was just buckling his seat belt when his phone buzzed. He picked it up, figuring it was Dad — he and Josh had been in touch all day.

But this time it was Greg.

Hey. You alive?

Barely, Josh wrote back, smiling as he pictured Greg's goofy grin. They'd been best buddies since preschool. Josh loved the guy, even if he could be a little dopey at times.

Like a couple of nights ago. They'd been playing video games in Josh's basement, wolfing down chips and Oreos. Suddenly Greg turned

17

to him and said, "Don't worry. I hear your dad probably won't have to go to jail for too long."

Josh had just stared at Greg, amazed that he could make such a dumb joke.

"I'm kidding," Greg said quickly.

"I know," Josh said. "But it's not funny."

Mom and Dad were still pretty upset about Dad getting arrested for no reason.

"I'm really sorry," Greg said, and for a second Josh was afraid Greg was going to start crying.

"Forget it," Josh said, giving Greg a friendly shove. He knew Greg wasn't trying to be mean. And why wreck a fun night?

Too bad Greg wasn't here with him now. This car ride would be way more exciting.

They texted back and forth about the Yankees until Greg had to go.

Don't have too much fun, Greg wrote.

Josh signed off with a googly-eyed, tongue-out emoji.

An hour later, Mom turned off the main street onto a skinny dirt road. They bumped along, driving deeper and deeper into the woods. Finally, they came to a small white house.

"How charming," Mom said as they stepped out of the car.

Josh guessed so. The house had a front porch with a picnic table and two rocking chairs. There were pots of flowers everywhere and all kinds of birds chirping and swooping around. It reminded Josh of a house from a kids' picture book. He half expected Goldilocks to come skipping out the front door.

They heard voices — a woman and a girl — echoing somewhere outside, in the back of the house.

"Why don't you grab the suitcases and bring them to the porch," Mom said to Josh. "I'll go find Holly and Nicole."

Josh hauled his duffel and Mom's suitcase up to the porch, then walked back to the car.

He looked around some more, squinting in the sun.

No basketball hoop. And he doubted there was a pool.

Josh's heart sank as he imagined the boring week ahead.

He fished his phone out of his pocket. He made a funny bored face and snapped a selfie for Dad.

Hi from the middle of nowhere, he typed. But then when he tried to send it, it wouldn't go through.

He stared at his phone screen — no cell service!

And that's when he heard it.

Hsssssssssss.

Josh swung his head around, and his heart stopped when he saw it: a massive lizard with brown-and-black speckled skin. It was at least six feet long, with a bullet-shaped head and a long tail. It looked like a leftover dinosaur or something.

Whatever it was, it was moving very fast, jaws open, teeth gleaming.

It was headed right for Josh.

CHAPTER 5

Josh turned and started running for his life.

"Stop!" a girl's voice shouted.

Josh stopped so suddenly he lost his balance. He fell forward, rolling onto the scratchy brown grass. Before he could scramble to his feet, the massive beast was there, its head right in front of Josh's trembling face. It glared at Josh through small, glowing yellow-brown eyes. Josh braced himself for the crunch of his nose being ripped from his face. He closed his eyes and held his breath.

One second passed. Two.

Ffffffftttt!

Something soft brushed against his cheek. Josh opened one eye.

Fffftttt!

A long skinny tongue — bubble-gum pink and forked at the end — came shooting out of the beast's mouth.

The tongue felt surprisingly soft on Josh's skin, like a feather.

The lizard batted its eyes at Josh.

Hello, friend, it seemed to say.

A girl with a curly brown hair came running up to Josh. He recognized Holly from the photo Mom had shown him. She was barefoot and wearing faded cutoff shorts and a T-shirt with a panda on it. A little red feather poked up from her hair.

Definitely a different type than Josh.

"Sorry," she said, smiling, as she caught her breath. "I doubt she would have bitten you. Savannah monitor lizards are usually pretty calm. But you never know."

Josh eyed the creature as he slowly stood up.

"I'm Holly." She grinned. "In case you hadn't figured that out." She pushed a curl away from her bright green eyes and pointed to the lizard. "And this beauty is Bubbles."

Bubbles?

And it dawned on Josh.

"That's . . . your . . . pet?"

COOL!

Wait until Greg and the guys heard about this. Dad had to buy Josh one! He'd name his giant lizard LeBron and take it on walks. Everyone at home would *freak*! Maybe Holly was cooler than he'd thought.

"No, no, no," Holly said, shaking her head. "Bubbles is not my pet. Nobody should be allowed to keep these amazing wild creatures as pets."

"So . . . where did you get her?" Josh asked.

"Someone bought her as a pet, then probably abandoned her in the forest," Holly said, looking sadly at Bubbles. "She would have died — lizards can't survive the winters here. But luckily someone found her and knew to call us. We run a little reptile shelter here, with a few of our friends."

A reptile shelter in their home?

Josh couldn't imagine that happening back in New Jersey.

"The animal shelter in town accepts dogs and cats, but not reptiles," Holly explained. "So we take them in — as long as they're not venomous or aggressive. We take care of them until we can find them good homes, like a wildlife refuge, or a zoo where they treat the reptiles really well."

That's a little . . . weird, Josh thought, *but pretty nice, too.*

Holly told Josh that monitor lizards like Bubbles were native to Africa and Indonesia. "They shouldn't be living anywhere near here," she said. "But you can buy pretty much anything online these days. Pythons, monitor lizards, anacondas. It's crazy. People don't realize that little pythons can grow to be twenty feet long, and cute baby lizards grow up to look . . . like Bubbles."

Bubbles lifted her head a little higher.

Aren't I gorgeous? she seemed to say.

Josh brushed his fingers across Bubbles's head, expecting it to be all slick and slimy. But her skin felt warm and surprisingly smooth, like an old football.

Fffffffftttt! She gave Josh another kiss, this time on his calf.

They walked toward the shade as Holly chattered away about different kinds of monitor lizards. This girl could *talk*. At least what she was saying was pretty interesting.

"Some monitor lizards are really aggressive," she went on. "But savannahs like Bubbles are calm. And super smart."

"Do you have other reptiles here right now?" Josh asked, looking around hopefully.

"Right now just Bubbles . . . and King Kong. He's a Burmese python."

"Those giant snakes?" Josh said.

Holly nodded. "He's about twelve feet long. Do you want to meet him?"

"Yes!" Josh said.

Bubbles scuttled behind them on her stubby legs, sticking close to Josh like a golden retriever. A golden retriever with scales. And a forked tongue. She was kind of . . . *cute*?

"She likes you," Holly said.

Pretty cool, Josh thought. Nobody would mess with a kid with a giant lizard as a friend.

They walked past a big vegetable garden and into a small garage.

Holly pointed out Bubbles's enclosure in the

back. It was a fenced-in area covered with sand, with branches and rocks and one of those plastic kiddie pools in the corner.

Across the garage was another enclosure, blocked off by a tall plexiglass gate.

"This is King Kong," Holly said, waving to the huge green-and-gold snake stretched across a log.

Josh took one look and nearly puked. Half the snake's skin was peeling off, like an old sock!

"What's the matter with him?" Josh gasped.

"Oh, he's just shedding his skin," Holy said. "All reptiles do it. Soon the old skin will come completely off. The skin underneath will be nice and healthy." She looked at the snake like she understood exactly how it felt. "It's not easy, though."

Josh made a face. He was glad he didn't have to shed *his* skin.

A minute later, Mom appeared with a tall woman wearing purple glasses. She had curly hair like Holly's, except with a few streaks of gray. Nicole, Josh realized.

"There you are!" Nicole said, rushing over to

Josh. She put an arm around him and grinned like they'd known each other forever. Mom was smiling, too — for the first time in days.

"Nice to meet you, Nic — Aunt Nicole," Josh decided. He knew they were technically cousins. But Nicole was pretty old, like Mom. At least forty. "Aunt Nicole" seemed right.

Josh's stomach let out a loud gurgle.

"Oh! You must be hungry!" Aunt Nicole said.

"Which is good," Holly said. "Because my mom's been baking for you for two days." She rolled her eyes and Josh laughed.

"I wasn't sure if you'd like brownies or muffins or chocolate chip cookies," Aunt Nicole said to Josh. "So I made them all."

"Awesome," Josh said. "Thanks!"

Josh looked around. This place was definitely a little . . . *different*.

But for the middle of nowhere, it didn't seem so bad.

CHAPTER 6

```
THREE NIGHTS LATER
FRIDAY, JULY 20, 2018
HOLLY'S HOUSE
AROUND 6:30 P.M.
```

Josh reached across the picnic table for another taco.

"Josh!" Mom laughed. "That's your third one!"

"Fourth," Josh said, smiling at Aunt Nicole. "These are the best tacos I've ever had."

A pink tongue shot up — *ffffffft!* — and snatched a piece of lettuce from the air as it tumbled from Josh's taco.

"Looks like Bubbles likes tacos, too," Mom said.

More laughter rose up, and a warm feeling spread from Josh's head to his toes. Mom had the right idea, to come out here. Josh missed Dad a ton. And it was weird not to be able to text Greg twenty times a day. But Mom was already back to her old self, and Josh felt calmer than he had in over a week.

He looked at Holly, who smiled at him over her taco. She was definitely different. Holly had never played a video game in her life. She could name every bird that flew by but not one basketball player.

"Who's that?" she'd asked the other day, pointing at the picture of LeBron James on Josh's T-shirt.

"You've never heard of LeBron James, the greatest player in the NBA?"

"I don't really care about basketball." Holly shrugged.

Josh just shook his head. Because what could he even say?

But somehow he and Holly got along. And surprisingly, it wasn't boring here, even without TV or video games or YouTube. He and Holly hung out with Bubbles and watched King Kong. They stuffed their faces with Aunt Nicole's brownies and cookies. And they spent the rest of the time roaming around the forest behind the house.

Hiking wasn't so bad, it turned out. Josh actually felt a little scared at first, being in the middle of a massive forest. He kept thinking of a movie he and Greg had watched, where two kids get lost for weeks. They stay alive by eating grasshoppers and moss.

But Holly knew her way around. They brought plenty of cookies and thermoses of lemonade. And sometimes they saw cool stuff, like a huge spider covered with fur, and a hawk flying overhead with a mouse gripped in its feet.

It was a bummer they weren't allowed to swim in the river; Holly said it was too dangerous to swim without a grown-up watching them. That really stank because there was an old zip line stretching across the river. It was attached to this big tree right on the riverbank. If Josh had a zip line in his backyard, he and Greg would be on it 24-7. Too bad Holly wasn't the zip-line type. She'd never even been on it!

Josh was finishing up his rice and beans when a dusty red pickup truck came zooming down the driveway.

"It's Lucas and Eleanor!" Holly exclaimed, rushing off the porch to greet the man and woman who got out.

"You'll love these two," Aunt Nicole said to Mom. "They're great friends of ours. They help us with the reptile shelter. Eleanor actually grew up with Hector."

Hector was Holly's dad, Josh knew. He'd died from cancer about three years ago, Mom had said. Holly had mentioned him a few times, her voice proud and sad at the same time. He seemed like a great guy.

Eleanor greeted Josh with a booming hello and a crushing hug. Lucas was quieter, but still super friendly.

"Join us for dinner!" Aunt Nicole said, clearing away space for two more plates.

But Eleanor shook her head. "We'd love to, but we're zonked. And we need a shower; we must stink of smoke."

"We just finished a shift at the fire station," Lucas added. "Four days on duty without a break."

Wow! Josh thought. Firefighters!

"And we have to go back for another shift tomorrow," Eleanor said. "We just stopped by to drop off a special supper for King Kong."

She held up a shoebox, wrapped in tape, with holes punched through the top. Josh could hear noises coming from inside the box.

Squeak squeak. Squeak.

"Nice big rat for his dinner," Lucas said. "Someone trapped it at the station, in our pantry."

Holly looked at Josh. "Pythons only eat live prey."

Josh winced. He wanted King Kong to have a good dinner. But it was too bad for the rat that snakes didn't like tacos.

"King Kong will love it," Holly said to Lucas. "He's having a tough time with his shedding."

"Well, hopefully this cheers him up," Lucas said. "I'll be right back." He took the box and headed to the garage.

Eleanor sat down with them at the table, and

Josh grabbed another taco. But he'd barely taken a bite when Lucas's voice rang out from the garage.

"Hey!" he called urgently. "Everyone come quick!"

They all stood up and raced toward the garage. Bubbles stuck close to Josh, following him like a scampering puppy.

Josh braced himself for a gruesome sight. He knew King Kong was chill. But Holly had told him some pythons could be dangerous. They weren't venomous like rattlesnakes or cobras. They killed their prey by squeezing them to death. Plus, they had strong jaws and sharp teeth.

They found Lucas standing in front of King Kong's enclosure, looking fine — no bite or strangle marks that Josh could see. But Lucas had a worried expression on his face.

"What is it?" Aunt Nicole asked, glancing around.

Lucas didn't answer. He just pointed into the enclosure.

Josh searched for the snake, but King wasn't

on his log. He wasn't lying on his bed of leaves, either.

Somehow, the massive python had vanished into thin air.

CHAPTER 7

"Look at this," Lucas called from the back corner of King's enclosure a few minutes later. "Loose board in the floor. King must have managed to pry it up with his head and slip out."

They got Bubbles into her enclosure and started the search for the snake. Josh used a rake to gently rustle the bushes around the garage. He squinted in the late-evening sun, knowing that King would be hard to spot. His dark-green-and-yellow-gold skin was an almost perfect match to the crunchy dried-up grass around the house.

Josh had moved on to some bushes on the far

side of the house when Aunt Nicole called them over to the bird feeder.

"I found something!" she shouted.

They gathered around her, and she held up what looked like a beige sock — a very long, very dry, very shriveled beige sock.

"King Kong finally shed his skin!" Holly said.

Aunt Nicole nodded. "I found it in the dirt, right over there."

"That's probably why he wanted to get out,"

Holly said. "When pythons are kept in captivity, it's harder for them to shed. They need to move across rough ground to get their skin off."

Josh's mind flashed to something Holly had told him about pythons, that in the wild they love to move around. Poor King had spent his whole life cooped up, first with his old owner and now in the pen in Holly's garage. Holly and Aunt Nicole took good care of him, but still. Josh's hands clenched tighter around his rake as he realized that Holly was right. It was cruel to keep these wild reptiles as pets.

Holly gently took the crinkly-looking skin from her mom. "I'm keeping this," she said.

Yikes, Josh thought. Snakes were cool, but keeping a snake skin would be like saving old toenails or something. He definitely wouldn't want the skin hanging around his house. Mom shot Josh a cringy look. She agreed.

Holly stashed King's skin in the garage and they searched for a little while longer. When it was dark enough that they had to use flashlights, Aunt Nicole called them all together.

"We're never going to spot King in the dark," she said. "My guess is he's found a hole, an animal burrow, to curl up in underground. Some rabbit or woodchuck is going to come home to a terrible surprise, but King will be safe. No animal around here would mess with a big python."

"But what about mountain lions?" Holly asked worriedly.

Josh's eyes went wide. "You have mountain lions here?!"

"They keep to themselves," Lucas said. "And I'm pretty sure a mountain lion would be smart enough not to bother King Kong."

As they made their way through the dusky darkness, Josh glanced over his shoulder at the forest, which seemed to stretch on forever.

King Kong was out there. Mountain lions, too.

What else was lurking in these woods?

He shuddered and walked a little faster toward the house.

CHAPTER 8

Aunt Nicole convinced Lucas and Eleanor to stay for dinner after all, and soon enough they were gathered around the picnic table. Lucas and Eleanor dug into some tacos and rice and beans. Everyone else helped themselves to some sweet and sticky flan for dessert. Aunt Nicole lit the small candles that were scattered across the table. They raised their glasses of lemonade and clinked to King Kong's safe return.

And then Mom turned her attention to Lucas and Eleanor.

"So tell us about your jobs," she said. "Must be exciting to be firefighters."

"We love it," Eleanor said, her eyes sparkling in the candlelight. "But for this time of year, it's a little *too* exciting. It's not even the hot part of fire season yet — that's not usually until August and the fall. But it's been so hot with no rain. The forests are dry as dust. We've already had some pretty big wildfires."

Josh paused mid-bite, thinking about the burned-out forest on their drive in. "You fight wildfires?" he asked. He'd been imagining them putting out house fires, like the firefighters in his town back home. But fighting wildfires? That sounded pretty amazing. Dad would definitely love meeting these two!

"That's right — they call us wildland firefighters," Lucas said, snagging a taco. "We work for Cal Fire — that's short for the California Department of Forestry and Fire Protection."

"Our air attack base is about ten miles from here," Eleanor added.

"Air attack?" Josh said. Sounded like the name of a new video game.

"Cal Fire has a small air force for fighting wildfires," Eleanor said, taking a scoop of rice and beans. "Twenty-two bases around the state, about one hundred aircraft. We're usually the first to the scene when a wildfire breaks out." She whipped out her phone, scrolled for a second, and held up a picture of a huge jet airplane.

"This is our DC-10 air tanker," she said. "This baby can fly over a fire and drop about twelve thousand gallons of water or flame retardant . . . that's the red stuff that makes it harder for a fire to spread."

Josh remembered from the video he saw how the plane seemed to be smearing red finger paint across the sky.

"And check this out," Eleanor said with a grin. "This is our Bell UH-1H Super Huey — finest helicopter there is, in my opinion. We use them to transport firefighters, to do water drops, and sometimes to rescue people."

Josh studied the picture of the red-and-white

helicopter. There was a person waving from the cockpit. He eyed Eleanor. "Is that you?" he asked.

Lucas smiled proudly. "Eleanor is one of the best pilots in the state."

"Awesome!" Josh blurted out, a little louder than he meant to. "I always wanted to ride in a helicopter."

Eleanor peeled back the sleeve of her T-shirt to show off a small helicopter tattoo on her shoulder.

Josh smiled, but then he imagined what it must be like to fly a helicopter into a fire. The idea terrified him.

"Don't you ever get . . . scared?" Mom asked, reading Josh's mind.

Eleanor nodded, swallowing a bite of taco. "All the time. But it's Lucas and the rest of the ground crew who take most of the risks, battling the fires up close. And some of these big fires we've been having lately . . ." She shook her head and looked at Lucas.

"They're definitely getting worse," he said. "Bigger. Hotter. Harder to control."

The candles flickered brighter.

"Is this because of climate change?" Mom asked.

Josh remembered the woman he and Mom had spoken to at the little store.

"Climate change is a huge part of it," Lucas said, picking up his glass of lemonade. "The summers are longer and hotter; the air is drier. But there are other reasons, too, like more and more people building houses in places that used to be wild. It used to be that lightning sparked most wildfires. But now it's people."

Eleanor nodded. "And our forests are unhealthy and overgrown, filled with dead trees. That's because in most places we haven't had *enough* wildfires, the small kind of fires that burn away the dead trees and dried-up brush."

"Why is that?" Mom asked.

"For about one hundred years, it's been our policy all over America to fight wildfires no matter what. That sounds smart, right? Protect our wilderness. But forests actually need wildfires to be healthy."

"I'm confused," Holly said, sitting back in her chair.

So was Josh. Weren't wildfires bad?

Lucas thought for a minute, then pointed to his plate, which was covered with rice and beans. "Imagine all this is a forest, with a mix of trees. Some are healthy, others are dead or sick, which is normal. If a fire starts in a forest like this, the flames take out the dead stuff — the sick trees, the dried-up brush. Most of the strong trees make it through." He pushed half of the rice and beans to the side of the plate, then spread out what was left. "So after the fire, what's left is healthier."

Eleanor leaned forward.

"Except, like I said, some of our forests haven't been allowed to burn for a hundred years. They're overloaded with dead and sick trees and dried brush. So now when a wildfire breaks out, there's so much more to burn. The fires get huge and so hot even most of the healthy trees don't stand a chance."

Josh stared at Lucas's plate. He got it.

"And in weather like this, all it takes is just one spark," Lucas said. "Yesterday some guy was smoking a cigar on a hiking trail — don't ask me why — and some ash dropped into the brush. Next thing you know, the whole hillside is in flames. Luckily we got there quick and knocked down the fire before it spread into the forest. If that had happened . . ." He just shook his head. "Disaster. That entire forest would have burned, and maybe the towns around it, too."

Josh flashed back again to those skeleton trees he and Mom had seen.

"On our way here from the airport we drove through a burned forest," he said.

"What a terrible sight," Mom added. "Just miles and miles of dead trees."

Lucas and Eleanor glanced at each other.

"That was the River Complex Fire — Cal Fire names the bigger wildfires," Lucas said. "That was one of the worst we've fought."

"You were in that?" Josh asked in amazement.

Eleanor nodded. "We barely made it out alive."

"You've never told us that story," Aunt Nicole said.

"I don't know . . ." Lucas said, shaking his head.

"I'd like to hear it," Josh said quickly, nodding.

Mom, Holly, and Aunt Nicole nodded, too.

So in the glow of the candles, Eleanor and Lucas told the story of that terrifying day.

CHAPTER 9

"It was July of 2015 — three years ago," Eleanor began. Her eyes filled with a faraway look, like in her mind she was traveling back to that day.

"A hiker had spotted a fire way up in the hills. She called 911, and they called us. In five minutes Lucas and the ground team were on board the helicopter — ten firefighters in all. I got them into the air and fifteen minutes later they were on the mountain, ready to go to work."

Lucas picked up from there. "Our job on the ground is to try to contain the fire, stop it from spreading. But when we're way up in a forest or far from roads, we don't have water or hoses — we can't drive our tanker trucks into the wild, and there aren't any fire hydrants.

"So we use chain saws and axes and saws to clear away trees and brush, scrape everything away down to the dirt. It's called building a fire line — a dirt path around the fire, maybe two or three feet wide." He picked up his fork again, and drew a circle around what was left of his rice and beans. "We're trying to take away the fuel the fire needs to spread.

"A wildfire's like a hungry animal. It feeds itself on things that will burn — trees, brush . . . that's its fuel. Take away its fuel, and the fire will weaken, then starve."

Like that time at basketball practice, Josh thought, *when I hadn't eaten breakfast.* He ran himself so hard he almost fainted. Greg practically had to carry him off the court.

"Most fires don't give us too much trouble," Lucas went on. "We put them out quickly. And at first, this River Complex Fire didn't worry us so much. Everything was calm. Then came the winds. Hot winds, very strong. They're called Santa Anas."

"*Diablo* winds," Eleanor said softly.

Josh shuddered. He knew from taking Spanish what *diablo* meant.

Devil.

"The winds whipped up the flames," Lucas said. "In ten minutes the fire had tripled in size. We could see it in the distance, that angry orange glow, getting bigger and brighter. The wind started to pick up big burning embers — chunks of wood and ash. These firebombs were landing all around us. I knew we had to get out of there, and quick. We radioed for help, and Eleanor came to pick us up."

Lucas's words were painting pictures in Josh's mind, pictures scarier than any video. He could see the flames. He could hear the *thwack, thwack, thwack* of the Huey helicopter and the roar of the wildfire. He could practically feel the hot wind blowing in his face.

"The main fire was still about a half mile away.

So I was able to land the Huey," Eleanor said. "Lucas and the team got on board. But now the winds were blowing at sixty, seventy miles per hour. Not even the Huey can take off in winds like that. The flames were closing in all around us. We were trapped."

Josh's heart hammered. He remembered when he and Mom were riding bikes one time, and a car swerved and hit Mom. She fell off her bike and badly hurt her leg. Josh had never felt so scared! But even if he multiplied that fear by ten, he didn't think it would come close to how it would feel to be in the middle of a wildfire — with no escape.

Lucas's voice dropped down. "In a wildfire like that, all you want to do is run. But when the flames are moving that fast, you usually can't outrun them. You have to try to find a big open space without trees or anything that can burn, like a ball field, or a big parking lot —"

"Or a river," Holly interrupted.

Eleanor smiled at Holly. "Smart kid. A wide

river can work like a fire line. But even that isn't always safe if the fires are too big and the winds are too strong. I've seen flames leap across a river. And the smoke can get so thick . . ."

"So what can you do?" Josh asked.

"At that point," Lucas said, "we knew the Huey would be lost. And our only hope was to use our fire shelters. We each keep one strapped to our backpacks, folded in a rectangle cube the size of a shoebox."

He told them how the fire shelters looked like very light sleeping bags or small thin tents. But they were made from fabric that could resist heat up to eight hundred degrees.

"You wrap the fire shelter around you, drop onto the ground on your stomach, and hold it tight so the fire doesn't rip it off when it goes over you."

Josh's mouth dropped open. "So you lie there . . . *inside* the fire?" He squirmed a little in his chair.

"That's right," Eleanor said.

"And the fire shelters work?" Mom asked.

"Most times," Lucas said. "But you have to make sure you're in a spot that's clean — just dirt or rock, no plants or grass around you that can burn. Because if the fire gets underneath you, the shelter will melt. Or even with just a small gap, the wind will tear off the shelter, and the hot gases . . ."

Everyone was very quiet for a moment.

"We weren't sure where we could go," Lucas continued. "Then I noticed some deer running down the hill. Squirrels and rabbits, too. Animals have a good instinct for where to go in a fire. We went in the same direction as them and were able to get to some clear land in time to deploy our fire shelters, and . . ."

His voice trailed off, and Eleanor picked up where he'd left off.

"We all dropped down and huddled together. We had just a few seconds before we heard the fire racing down the mountain toward us. The sound . . . it's like a jet plane is coming in for a landing, right on your head. Then the flames are on top of you. The fire sucks the air out of your lungs, burns your throat. You feel like you're being cooked alive. All you want to do is get up and run. But if you do . . ."

Josh closed his eyes and forced his brain to go blank. He couldn't think about what it would be like to be belly-down on the ground while a fire roared on top of him.

"How long did you have to stay like that?" Mom asked softly.

"A minute, maybe less," Lucas said. "Felt like hours. But then it was over."

"How terrible," Mom whispered.

"It was," Lucas said. "We've been through some bad fires. But that one still gives me nightmares."

Eleanor nodded.

"But something happened to our team that day," she said. "We came together. Got each other through. And now . . . it almost feels . . ." Her voice trailed off, like she wasn't sure how to explain how she felt.

"Like we're tied together," Lucas picked up. "Like there's an invisible rope connecting us, always."

Eleanor smiled. "That's exactly how it feels."

Josh knew that feeling. It was like after a tough basketball game, when he and Greg and the guys had fought for every point. The team always felt super close afterward.

They finished up their dinner, everyone a little quieter, and said goodbye to Lucas and Eleanor.

Later that night, when Josh was trying to fall asleep, the fire shelter story kept replaying in his mind.

To be *inside* a wildfire and survive — it seemed impossible.

But he'd just met people who had done it.

CHAPTER 10

Josh woke up early Monday. Mom was still fast asleep in the bed next to his. Josh eyed his duffel bag, which sat on the floor, almost all packed. He and Mom were leaving today at noon, driving to the airport and flying back to New Jersey.

Holly had helped Josh pack last night.

"Bubbles is going to miss you," she'd said,

folding one of Josh's T-shirts. "I think she might hide in your suitcase."

"I'd love that," Josh said, smiling as he pictured a giant lizard tail sticking out of the duffel. "But I might have a problem going through airport security."

That cracked them both up.

He was definitely going to miss Bubbles, Josh thought now as he tossed around in the bed. And he already missed King — the snake still hadn't shown up.

But Josh also couldn't wait to get back to his real life. He wanted to see Dad, shoot hoops with Greg, jump into their pool.

He lay there a few minutes more, already dreading the endless drive to the airport. Finally he slid out of bed. He figured he'd go get Bubbles and wait on the porch for everyone to get up.

Josh threw on his clothes and went downstairs to the kitchen. Aunt Nicole had baked blueberry muffins last night. He grabbed one and took a bite — *crazy good!* — then stuffed the whole thing into his mouth. He was helping himself to a second muffin when he spotted Aunt Nicole's laptop sitting open on the table.

He eyed it, thinking about the Yankees. Had he really not checked his scores in a whole week?

He sat down at the table and brushed the crumbs from his fingers. He knew Aunt Nicole wouldn't mind if he used her computer for a minute. A few clicks later, he was scrolling through the scores.

Yes! The Yanks had creamed the Red Sox last night.

He checked on a few more games. And then, almost without thinking, he googled Dad's name. He was sure no one was writing those garbage articles anymore.

That's why he almost choked on his muffin as he saw the headline of the first article:

Tim Wallace, New Jersey Banker, Sentenced to 8 Months in Jail

Josh laughed out loud.

What a joke! If anyone should go to jail, it was whoever wrote these lies!

But then Josh saw where this article was from: the *New York Times*.

The *New York Times* was not a trashy newspaper. Mom and Dad always said it was the best newspaper in the world. What was going on?

Josh started to read the article. But then he heard voices — Mom, Aunt Nicole, Holly. Everyone was awake and heading downstairs. Almost without thinking, Josh pushed away from the table and hopped up. He rushed into the little bathroom off the kitchen and gently shut the door.

Voices filled the kitchen.

"Pancakes or omelets?" Aunt Nicole asked.

The fridge opened and shut.

"Josh likes pancakes," Holly said.

"Where *is* Josh?" Mom said. "I thought he'd be down here."

"Two muffins are missing," Aunt Nicole said with a laugh. "So we know he's come through here."

"I bet he's with Bubbles," Holly said. "I'll go get him."

The screen door squeaked open, then slammed closed.

Sweat trickled down Josh's back — it was broiling in this little bathroom. He had to get out of here. He was about to flush the toilet, to make it seem he'd been in here for a reason. But then he heard Aunt Nicole gasp.

"Trish. Come over here."

"What?" Mom said.

"This article in the *New York Times*. It's about Tim. It was up on my computer . . ."

Josh froze. He realized he'd left the article open on the screen.

"The article is from this morning," Aunt Nicole said. "Someone must have been using my computer before we came down."

"You think it was Josh?" Mom said, her voice dropping down.

Josh's whole body started to tingle, like when that car hit Mom on her bike. And when he saw Dad being taken away in handcuffs.

It got very quiet — the only sound was a fly

buzzing around the window. Josh pictured Mom and Aunt Nicole huddled around the computer.

"I have to call Tim," Mom finally said, her voice filled with worry. "We were going to tell Josh everything when we got back."

Tell me everything? Josh thought. That meant Mom *hadn't* been telling Josh the whole story so far.

He thought back to Greg's dumb joke. *Your dad probably won't have to go to jail for too long.*

Maybe he hadn't been joking at all. Maybe he had known something Josh did not.

Suddenly, Josh didn't know what to believe.

He took a breath, braced himself, and slowly opened the bathroom door. When he stepped into the kitchen, Aunt Nicole jumped a little, like Josh had popped out of a cabinet.

"Is it true, what that article says?" Josh asked Mom. His voice was louder than he meant it to be, and it cracked a little. "Dad really did steal that money?"

"Josh . . ." Mom said, standing up and stepping toward him. "He didn't steal the money.

He broke some laws, yes. But it's not what you think."

"Is he going to jail?" Josh asked.

"Let's call Dad," Mom answered. "He'll explain everything. You'll see . . ."

"Just tell me, Mom," Josh said, fighting tears. "Is Dad going to jail?"

Mom's voice dropped to a whisper.

"Yes," she said. "He is."

CHAPTER 11

The next thing Josh knew, he was out the door, sprinting across the lawn. He heard Mom calling after him. Holly stepped out of the garage as Josh rushed past.

"Josh! You won't believe it! King Kong! He's back! I walked into the garage . . ."

But Josh kept running, not even looking at her.

"Where are you going?" she shouted after him.

He dashed across the big grassy yard, down the hill, and finally into the forest. He followed one of the hiking trails.

Faster! he told himself, brushing through the

scratchy pine branches that lined the path, jumping over a dead branch. *Faster!*

But it didn't matter how fast he was going. He couldn't escape the ugly truth.

Dad — his hero — was a criminal.

Josh ran until he couldn't take another step. He was so far into the woods; he couldn't see the house through the trees. This was farther than he and Holly had ever come before. He staggered to a stop and dropped to the ground between two big pine trees. He sat there, gasping for breath.

His mind swirled.

That whole story about a computer glitch at the bank — it was a lie.

This trip to California. It was all a big trick.

Mom hadn't dragged Josh here for an exciting adventure. They came here because this was the middle of nowhere. Because it was one of the only places Mom could take him where Josh would be cut off from everything — the news, texts from friends, the truth.

Josh was so lost in his thoughts that he didn't hear Holly's footsteps. But now here she was in front of him, her face shiny with sweat. She tried to catch her breath.

Josh turned away. *She must have known the truth, too*, Josh thought. She and Aunt Nicole were probably in on the whole thing.

"Please just go," Josh said, wiping his tears and waving her away. "I want to be by myself."

He still couldn't believe Dad had stolen that money! How was that possible? How could his father be a criminal?

Josh pictured Dad taking care of Mom after

her bike accident, carrying her up the stairs, cooking her favorite foods. Dad's bright, strong voice rang through Josh's mind, cheering Josh on in the driveway while he was practicing his three-pointers. He saw Dad's big smile, the one that made Josh feel he could do anything.

Now it seemed that person was gone.

Holly came closer.

"Josh," she pleaded. "What's going on? Are you okay? Are you mad at me? Did I do something?"

Josh studied her. She looked totally confused, her face one big question mark. Could it be that she really didn't know the truth about his dad?

Holly sat down in the dirt next to Josh. Her eyes searched his face for answers.

Josh decided that no, Holly wasn't faking. They'd spent almost every minute together over the last week. He doubted she could keep such a big secret the whole time.

So Josh spat it all out — the whole ugly story about Dad. The arrest. The lies. The *New York Times* article. "He's going to jail," Josh finally said.

Holly's eyes widened. "Jail?"

Josh nodded.

His shock was fading, he realized. Now he was just sad. Sadder than he'd ever been.

"Did you hear King came back?" Holly said, definitely trying to distract him. "It was the weirdest thing. I walked into the garage looking for you, and there he was, wrapped around his log. Like he'd never left."

She smiled hopefully, but Josh turned away. He was happy about King, of course. But he was pretty sure he'd never want to smile again.

They sat there for what seemed like a long time, staring up into the trees. Finally Holly moved closer to him.

"When my dad died, everything changed," she said in a very soft voice. "We used to live in the city. My mom worked as a lawyer. I went to this fancy school."

Josh looked at her.

"Really?" Josh said. It was impossible to imagine Holly living anywhere other than here.

"Eleanor was an old friend of my dad's," Holly said. "She was living here, and convinced me and my mom to move. I hated it here at first. I just wanted my old life back."

She paused for a few seconds.

"But I got used to things, after a while. It wasn't easy, to start over. But I did it. It was like . . . like shedding my skin." She looked at Josh. "You know?"

No, Josh thought, *I don't know.* Sometimes Holly said things he just didn't get. And before she could say more, her eyes suddenly went wide. She scrambled to her feet and looked around.

"What's wrong?" Josh asked. That expression on Holly's face. It scared him.

"Do you smell that?" she said, her nose twitching.

"What?" he said.

Holly looked at Josh.

"Smoke."

CHAPTER 12

Josh stood up, too, and sniffed the air. Yes, he smelled it. Just barely.

"Could it be a campfire?" he asked. He pictured a group of Boy Scouts sitting outside their tents, cooking up their morning eggs and sausages.

Holly shook her head.

"Nobody is supposed to be having campfires now, anywhere. Not with the fire risk so high." Her eyes flicked back and forth. "There's a wildfire somewhere."

Josh's heart thumped.

Holly looked all around and up at the sky, and Josh followed her gaze. But it was impossible to see anything because they were in the middle of this forest. The trees towered up over them, blocking their view of the sky and everything around.

"It's probably not close to here," Holly said. "We smell smoke all the time. It could be from a fire ten miles away."

Josh nodded, praying that was it.

Holly gave the air another big sniff. "It's not getting stronger, is it?"

Josh raised his nose up, breathing in. "I don't think so," he said. The smell hadn't disappeared, but he didn't think it was getting stronger, either. It was about the same.

"Good," Holly said. "Let's just get back."

Josh wasn't going to argue with that.

They headed down the skinny path in the direction of Holly's house. The pine trees towered over them. Their footsteps crunched on the brush and dried-up pine needles that covered the ground.

Holly's eyes were fixed ahead, and Josh's

71

thoughts swung back to Dad. To home. By now everyone in his town must know that Dad was going to jail.

How could he and Mom go back there? What kind of life would they have?

Suddenly, the hot wind gusted hard, drying up the tears that had sprung into Josh's eyes. Something landed on his head. Instantly he felt a searing pain, like he'd been stung by a giant wasp.

"Ouch!" he cried, brushing the thing off his head and onto the ground. It wasn't a buzzing insect. It was a small chunk of burned tree bark, glowing red. He and Holly stared as it landed on a pile of dried-up twigs and brown pine needles.

Whoosh!

The dried brush immediately caught fire.

Holly lunged at the low, flickering flame like it was her worst enemy. She stamped on it with her tattered running shoes until it was out.

"You see any more?" she said, swiveling all around.

Josh shook his head.

"Whew," Holly said. She let out a big breath.

What was *that?* Josh wondered.

And then he remembered what Lucas has said the other night, that big wildfires give off burning bits of wood — embers — that blow in the wind and set new fires.

So the wildfire they were smelling . . . it couldn't be very far away.

Josh had the creeped-out feeling that that ember had been sent out to find them, a flaming eyeball flying through the sky. *I'm watching you.*

"Come on," Holly said.

They walked more quickly now. And for the first time, Josh looked closely at the forest around them. He thought of what Eleanor had said — that some forests were in bad shape. Now he saw what she meant. The trees were all crammed together, branches tangled up. Lots of the trees looked sick — too small and too skinny, bark peeling off, with branches spindly and bare. And every inch of the ground was covered with fallen limbs, weedy-looking bushes, and dried-up pine needles.

He thought of how quickly that one little

ember had ignited that patch of ground. A chill went up his spine. But he stopped himself from panicking.

This is California, he reminded himself, *not New Jersey.* Wildfires were normal here, and most of them were put out quickly. Hadn't Lucas and Eleanor said that? It was like the snowstorms at home. Every few winters there was a monster blizzard that shut everything down. But mostly they got a few inches of powdery snow, not even enough for a snow day from school.

Josh had just about calmed himself down when a strange sound rose from behind them. A low growl.

He and Holly both froze. They locked eyes, then slowly turned around.

A mountain lion was crouched on the path behind them.

CHAPTER 13

Josh's mouth dropped open, but he was too shocked to make a sound.

Holly grabbed his hand.

"Don't move," she whispered.

Even from twenty feet away, Josh could see muscles bulging under the mountain lion's short golden fur.

She stared at them. Then she let out a bone-rattling scream.

Yeooooooooowwwwww!

Josh's blood turned to ice as the mountain lion exploded off the ground and came charging toward them. Josh grabbed hold of Holly, pushing her out of the lion's path. Or maybe it was Holly who grabbed him and pulled. Still, Josh braced himself for the slashing claws, for the knife-sharp teeth.

But the lion raced right past them, a golden blur. Josh met her eyes as she flew by. The animal didn't look ferocious or vengeful.

She looked terrified.

Just then, a huge flock of birds zoomed overhead.

Four squirrels raced by.

All the animals were heading in the same direction as the mountain lion.

Holly's face lit up at the sight of all the animals. But her expression changed to terror as a new sound — a crackling roar — rose up around them. This time Josh knew it wasn't an animal.

They both turned, and Josh saw it — a bloodred glow in the distance, getting bigger by the second.

He and Holly both stared, hardly believing what they were seeing.

The wildfire. It had found them.

The glow got bigger until it looked more like a wall — a wall of flames that was moving right toward them.

"Josh! Run!" Holly screamed. She grabbed his hand.

They took off. But they had barely taken ten steps when they were hit by a powerful gust of hot wind. And suddenly there were embers everywhere — burning sparks and flaming chunks of bark and wood. They swarmed all around them.

Josh let go of Holly's hand and flung his hands wildly, brushing the embers away. The attack went on, though, the embers biting into his skin like the needle-sharp teeth of a flaming monster.

But it wasn't his or Holly's flesh that the embers were really after. It was the tinder-dry trees, the fallen branches and piles of dried-up pine needles. The embers showered down, greedily taking hold, setting fires wherever they landed.

On treetops.

WHOOSH!

On branches.

WHOOSH!

On the forest floor.

WHOOSH!

Josh and Holly began running down the path again. They zigzagged from one side of the path to the other whenever a new fire whooshed to life in their way. With every gust of wind, that giant wall of flames raced closer to them. And the noise . . .

A nightmare of sounds pummeled Josh's ears. The fire's roar, the moaning wind, the cracking and snapping and hissing of the burning trees. The sound was louder than any plane or train. It was as though the air itself were shrieking in agony.

Three deer shot by them, diagonally off the trail. Holly grabbed Josh's arm.

"Josh! Let's follow them!"

Josh remembered what Lucas had said, about animals and wildfires.

That lion — she must have sensed the fire coming this way before Holly and Josh had. Those other animals, too. And now these deer . . . maybe they knew the best route to escape.

"They're heading for the river!" Holly said.

The river! Josh thought. *Smart deer!*

They took off into the trees. Maybe that wall of flames wouldn't be able to follow them across the river. It was a natural fire line, like Lucas and Eleanor had described. And the cool water would protect Josh and Holly from the embers.

They ran faster.

And then:

Boom!

A tree in front of them exploded. The wood splintered and shards sprayed out. Holly tried to pull him sideways. But his hand slipped out of hers. He looked up just in time to see a flaming limb sailing through the air, taking aim at his skull.

CHAPTER 14

Josh snapped his head to the side, avoiding the full-on hit.

But as the branch sailed by him, a paper-sized strip of burning tree bark dropped onto his arm. Pain exploded through his body like an electric shock as the bark burned through his skin.

"Aaaaaaaaaaaaahhhhhh!" Josh screamed, falling to the ground. It felt as if the bark had glued itself to his flesh. Before he could think twice, he reached up and peeled it off his skin. He threw the bark on the forest floor. It crackled and hissed like a rabid rat.

And now his fingers were burned, too.

Josh sat there, dazed and shaking. The pain was like none he'd ever felt, as if the flesh of his arm had been roasted, ripped from the bone. His fingers throbbed as if he'd pricked himself with a thousand needles. He wanted to curl up into a ball, let the pain crash over him. To disappear inside it.

But now Holly was next to him. She stomped on the hissing bark so it wouldn't ignite the brush on the ground. She reached down and grabbed Josh's hand, not realizing he'd been burned.

He pulled it away, crying out in pain.

"My hand is burned," Josh said. "And my arm."

"We can't stop," Holly said. "Come on."

Josh wanted to move. But the pain was making him feel sick and dizzy. He was sure he couldn't stand up, let alone run.

But Holly gently took his other hand and managed to pull him to his feet. She stood there for a few seconds, very close.

"I know it hurts," she said. "But you can do it."

She sounded almost like Dad.

Somehow Josh forced his body forward. And soon he was running again. He followed close to Holly, his eyes stinging from the smoke and ash. They zigzagged around the burning branches and puddles of flame on the ground.

The sky was filled with birds flying away from the fire. And other animals were on the run, too. A rabbit hopped in front of them. Chipmunks and squirrels skittered at their feet.

"The river's not far!" Holly shouted, coughing from the smoke. "It's just over the hill. We're almost there!"

The temperature was rising — the air was searing hot, the ground a stovetop that burned Josh's feet through his sneakers and socks. He could practically feel his blood boiling inside his veins.

How much heat could the human body stand? He had no idea. But he could tell he wasn't going to last much longer. His skin was roasting. Each breath of the smoky air seared his throat and lungs. And it would only be a few minutes before the wall of flames caught them.

They kept up their desperate climb.

"We made it!" Holly said as they reached the top of the hill. But then she gasped.

"*No!*"

Right in front of them, blocking the river, was a line of blazing bushes — a fence of fire. Josh turned his head. The flames seemed to stretch out for hundreds of feet in both directions.

They were trapped.

Josh thought of the fire shelters Lucas had described. If only they had one of those!

But they had nothing to protect them.

Suddenly a deer came barreling from behind them. It launched itself over the bushes and hit the water.

Splash!

Holly stared at the deer, then turned to Josh. "The zip line! We're close to the zip line!"

"Zip line?" he said, wondering if the smoke was messing with her head.

"It could take us over those bushes. We can let go over the river and swim across. Like the deer!"

She whipped her head around, eyes narrowed and searching.

"There it is!" She pointed to the zip line.

It was a crazy idea.

And their *only* idea.

In a flash they were on the move again. But now all Josh could think of was what could go wrong. The path to the tree could be blocked. Even if they got there, the zip-line tree could be burned. The wire could have melted in the heat. And how would he be able to hold on with his burned hand?

He tried to push those fears from his mind as Holly led them farther over the hill. They had to keep changing direction, to zigzag around the flaming trees and branches in their path.

"There," Holly said finally, pointing to a big tree.

He couldn't imagine how she'd managed to find it. But there it was. Josh saw the zip-line wire stretching across the river.

There were some embers clinging to the tree's branches. But somehow it was not on fire.

Josh almost cried with relief.

"Follow me," Holly said, hoisting herself up onto the lowest branch. Josh scrambled right behind her, gutting through the pain of his burns.

He noticed that this tree wasn't an evergreen like most of the others. It didn't have spindly branches covered with pine needles. Its leaves were big and bright green, the branches strong. Its bark was very thick, like armor. He thought of what Lucas had told them, that some trees were strong and shaded, holding enough moisture to withstand fires. He hoped this one could last at least a few seconds longer.

They reached the branch where the zip line was attached. The zip line seemed old — it had a worn-down wooden handle. There were leaves and twigs stuck in it. Would it even work?

Holly brushed off the leaves and took hold of the handle.

"We have to go at the same time," she said.

Josh nodded. There was no time to take turns.

They locked eyes.

They both knew how dangerous this was.

What if the heat had weakened the wire and it snapped before they were over the line of bushes?

And the smoke was so thick. They couldn't see across the river. For all they knew, the fires on the other side were as bad — or worse. They'd be trapped in the middle of the river, suffocating in the smoke.

Josh took a breath. He reached up. His arm throbbed. Pain stabbed through his hand as he curled his fingers around the handle next to Holly's.

"Go!" Holly said.

CHAPTER 15

They pushed off and started to fly. They whizzed along the wire. The burning bushes seemed to reach up for them. But the wire held. In seconds, he and Holly were over the river.

"Let go NOW!" Holly cried.

Josh opened his fingers and fell through the smoke.

SPLASH!

He could practically hear the hiss of his hot body hitting the cold river. And he knew that for as long as he lived, he would never forget the feeling of this cool water on his roasted skin. He let himself sink down, down, down, where the embers couldn't reach him, where the fire's roar was muffled.

But his aching lungs couldn't hold much air. Only a few seconds later he was back on the surface, gulping in smoky breaths. Embers swirled around, glowing bits of wood, some ribbons of flaming bark. A few landed on him and he splashed them away.

The smoke wasn't as thick down here near the water. He could see some small fires on the other side of the river. But nothing compared to what they'd escaped. The current was strong. But not as strong as in the ocean at the Jersey Shore, where Josh had learned to swim. He could handle it.

His hopes rose up.

He looked for Holly, surprised she wasn't shouting out her orders. Where was she? He spun around, searching. Had she already started swimming to the other side?

No. She wouldn't go without him. He saw some pieces of wood floating in the water. But no sign of his cousin.

"Holly!" he called.

He swam back and forth, swinging his head around. His eyes kept returning to what looked like a rock, bobbing in the water. But wait . . . rocks don't float. That was Holly!

He thrashed over to her and grabbed hold of her arms under the water. He tried to pull her up, but she was stuck!

Josh took a breath and dove down. He groped in the water; her leg was caught in a branch. It took him three dives before he could work her leg free. He wrapped his arms around her and pulled her to the surface. They both exploded up out of the water.

He'd done it!

But Holly was strangely silent. Her head lolled. "Holly!" he screamed. "Holly!"

But she didn't open her eyes.

CHAPTER 16

Josh's mind swirled in panic as he bicycled his legs under the water, desperately trying to keep them both afloat. In health class, he'd learned what to do if someone was choking. Was drowning the same as choking? It didn't matter — it was the only thing he could think to do.

He managed to whip Holly around so her back was against his chest. He wrapped his arms around her, locked his hands under her rib cage, and pushed in hard right below her chest.

Water gushed from her mouth. She sputtered

and gulped in the smoky air, coughing between each breath. Her eyes fluttered open.

But something still wasn't right.

"My leg," Holly said weakly. "I think it's broken. I can't move it."

Josh struggled to hold her up.

He kept his eyes on the fires on the opposite side of the river. They were growing bigger now. If he and Holly didn't get over there soon, they would lose any chance of getting out alive. A feeling of doom rose up inside Josh.

But so did something else: a rush of energy. Like at that basketball game, when they were down by two and time was running out. When there had been nobody to pass to and it was up to him to try to make that three-point shot.

Josh whirled around in the water so his back was to Holly.

"Climb on!" Josh shouted, the words coming out before he knew he was saying them. "I'll get us to the other side."

Holly had gotten them through the flames, to the river, over the burning trees. She'd picked him up when he was hurt, cheered him on when he was sure he couldn't move.

Now it was his turn.

Holly wrapped her arms around his neck. Then Josh started to swim.

It was hard. Really hard. Josh had to kick his legs and stroke very fast with his one good arm. It took every ounce of strength he had to keep them afloat. But he did it. Inch by inch, he moved them forward until finally his feet scraped the river bottom.

He held Holly on his back and staggered toward the shore. He made it to knee-deep water and then couldn't go another step. The pain in his arm and hand was agonizing. His legs were shaking. The smoke made it almost impossible to breathe.

"I just . . . need . . . to . . . rest . . . for a minute," he gasped.

But the new fires were gaining power. Flames hopped from one tree to the next. Embers took hold.

WHOOSH!
WHOOSH!

WHOOSH!

"We can't stay here," Holly said, reading Josh's mind.

"There," Josh said, pointing about thirty yards up, where the trees and bushes were farther back from the river. "It's better up there."

Josh turned so Holly could climb onto his back.

He staggered forward, praying his legs wouldn't give out.

The fire roared and crackled and shrieked. And then there was a new sound, a furious pounding from behind them.

Thwack. Thwack. Thwack.

The noise reminded Josh of a ferocious beast snapping its jaws. He imagined a huge creature bursting through the wall of fire, its jagged teeth gleaming through the black smoke. He was afraid to turn around.

The river began to churn. The hot wind swirled faster, whipping around them.

And whatever was making the sound got closer.

THWACK. THWACK. THWACK.

"Josh," Holly rasped into his ear. Her voice was bright, not scared. "Look!"

Josh glanced back.

And sure enough, something enormous hovered behind them.

But it wasn't a fiery beast.

It was a helicopter — white and red.

Josh's heart leaped.

The Huey!

CHAPTER 17

The helicopter hovered low, in the middle of the river, its bright light slicing through the thick smoke. A big door opened and someone leaped out, splashing down into the water. Seconds later Josh heard a voice, shouting through the darkness.

"JOSH! HOLLY!"

"LUCAS!!!" Holly called.

Lucas waded toward them. He wrapped his arms around both of them, hugging them close.

"Come on," he said. "We don't have much time."

"Holly hurt her leg," Josh said quickly.

"What about you?" he asked Josh.

"His shoulder's burned. Bad," Holly said.

"But I can make it," Josh said, surprising himself.

The helicopter had moved closer to them at the edge of the river, still hovering, the sound of the rotor blades beating like a giant heart. A stretcher was lowered down, attached to a cable.

Lucas strapped Holly into the stretcher and waved to Josh to wait.

"I'm going to take her up and be right back down for you!" he shouted into Josh's ear. "Hang tight!" And up Lucas and Holly went.

Josh understood — Holly was badly hurt. But the feeling of being left behind hurt more than his burns. And it seemed like hours before Lucas came back down for him.

Lucas quickly hooked Josh into what looked like a big vest.

"This is a screamer suit!" Lucas shouted into his ear. "You'll be nice and secure for the ride."

And seconds later he and Lucas were rising toward the Huey.

Josh looked around. The flames on this side of the river were getting even bigger, shooting high into the sky. Josh imagined those flames reaching all the way to the moon, setting it on fire.

The hot wind gusted harder, making Josh and Lucas swing wildly. More trees were exploding.

BOOM!

BOOM!

BOOM!

And then a vicious gust seemed to grab hold of the Huey, twisting it sideways. The helicopter lurched, and Josh squeezed his eyes shut.

Please, he thought. *Please don't let this helicopter crash on top of us.*

The old helicopter held steady in the air. And finally they were at the open door. There was a firefighter waiting for them. He plucked Josh out first, then helped Lucas climb inside. The door slammed.

Within seconds, Josh was strapped into a seat next to Holly in her stretcher. Holly's face was tense with pain. Her eyes were squeezed shut and tears rolled down her cheeks. Josh's burns throbbed. But he could tell Holly's pain was much worse.

Eleanor looked at them from the pilot's seat, her face steely.

"Hold tight!" she bellowed. "I'm getting us out of here!"

The Huey moved forward for a few seconds, its nose dipping down as it gained speed. Then it shot up so fast, Josh's stomach flipped. He thought of all the times he'd wished he could fly in a helicopter. But not in a million years could he have imagined a ride like this. Next to him, Holly opened her eyes and turned toward the window.

"Look," she whispered.

The smoke around them had parted. And what Josh saw made his eyes fill up with tears. Flames shot up on both sides of the river. The burning trees twisted in the wind, branches waving wildly, like they were begging for help. Josh wished they could rescue all of them, carry them away.

Soon there would be almost nothing left down

there, Josh knew. Just skeleton trees, bent and broken and still. Burned to ash.

He leaned closer to Holly and grabbed her hand.

The Huey rose higher where the smoke was thicker, and then there was nothing more to see.

Josh closed his eyes, suddenly more tired than he'd ever been. His body felt numb.

All he could feel was Holly's hand in his, holding him tight.

CHAPTER 18

ABOUT THREE WEEKS LATER
HOLLY'S HOUSE

Flames were everywhere; trees were exploding. Josh ran as fast as he could, but it was no use. He fell onto his back. And then . . .

Fffffffft.

Fffffffft.

Josh's eyes shot open.

Bubbles had her head resting on the bed, inches from Josh's face.

Fffffffft.

The lizard licked him again, then made a purring sound. *Wake up!*

Josh's heart was still pounding. He wondered how long he'd be having these nightmares.

A long time, he guessed.

He rested his hand on Bubbles's smooth head.

"Good morning," he said.

Fffffffft. A kiss on his chin.

He looked around — the sun was shining bright outside. Mom's bed was neatly made, her suitcase all packed.

"Bubbles?" Holly's voice called out. "Where are you?"

A minute later she came in, hobbling on her crutches. It was good to see her moving around, not wincing with every step.

"You know the rule," Holly scolded when she spied Bubbles. "No lizards upstairs!"

Bubbles let out an insulted little hiss and scuttled out.

Josh and Holly both shook their heads and laughed. But then they went quiet. Holly eyed Mom's suitcase.

"I wish you could stay," Holly said.

"Me too," Josh said, his throat tightening.

He and Holly looked at each other, and Josh got a lump in his throat.

She sure was different from him. But something had happened to them in that fire. Like what Lucas and Eleanor had said happened to them and the rest of their crew after the River Complex Fire. He and Holly had come together. They'd gotten each other through. And now it felt like they were tied together somehow.

And it was different from how he felt after a good game with his basketball buddies. Basketball was important to him, but it was just a sport. That feeling of togetherness he and the guys felt after a big win didn't last between games.

This tie with Holly? Josh knew it would last forever.

Aunt Nicole's voice echoed up the stairs. "Holly! Josh! Breakfast!"

"It's your goodbye feast," Holly said. "Mom's been cooking since dawn."

They laughed, and Holly left him to get dressed.

The smell of muffins and bacon pulled Josh out of bed. His stomach growled. Finally he had his appetite back. And he could swallow. Breathing in all that smoke had hurt his throat. And his lungs. He and Holly had both been in bad shape.

After the Huey landed at the air attack base, they'd been rushed to the hospital. Holly needed surgery on her broken leg. The burn on Josh's arm was deep, and doctors had to take skin from his leg and put it onto his arm. His hand needed treatment, too. For days they both wore oxygen masks to help them breathe. They were still using inhalers three times a day.

But they were both getting stronger. And finally the doctors had said Josh was well enough to make the trip home to New Jersey. Mom had booked their flights a couple of days ago.

Josh got dressed. He tied his sneakers, staring at the nasty burn scars on his arm and fingers. At least they didn't hurt so much anymore.

Josh got up and looked out the window. The

part of the forest behind the house was still green — the winds had shifted and carried the flames away. That's the only reason this house was still here. That last-minute change in the wind.

The fire — named the Carr Fire — had spread far and was still burning in some places. More than a thousand firefighters from around the state and the country were battling it, including Eleanor and Lucas.

Firefighters were starting to get it under control, but the fire was still dangerous. It had already destroyed nearly two hundred thousand acres. It had spread into the big town of Redding and burned a thousand houses. Eight people had died.

Meanwhile, another huge fire had broken out north of here.

2018 was already one of the worst fire years in California history.

And as Lucas had said, it wasn't even the busy time of fire season yet.

After breakfast, Mom and Aunt Nicole loaded the car. Josh and Holly went to say goodbye to

King Kong. The big snake had returned to his enclosure the same way he'd escaped, through the little hole in the floor. (And right after he returned, Aunt Nicole had fixed the floor!)

Josh stood and watched King as he wrapped himself around his log, his green-and-gold skin glistening in the sun. Finally Josh waved goodbye to the snake, and walked to Bubbles's enclosure. He stepped inside and bent down for one last lizard kiss.

Ffffffft.

Bubbles let out a low purr. *Good luck,* she seemed to say. Josh didn't mind that Holly could see his tears.

He and Holly headed slowly to the car. Aunt Nicole wrapped Josh up in one of her crushing hugs. Then she handed him a heavy bag. "You've got a few dozen cookies, brownies, and muffins. That should last you until you get to New Jersey."

"Or the airport," Holly joked.

"We're going to need extra snacks," Mom said. "I hear there's lots of traffic because of the fires."

Josh groaned to himself as he thought of the endless ride. Then again, he didn't really want to get home, either.

Josh gave Holly one last hug and then he and Mom got into the car.

"There's a present for you," Holly said to Josh, pointing toward the back seat, to a shoebox tied with white ribbon. "From me. Open it when you're on the road."

Mom started the car and they pulled away.

"See you for Thanksgiving!" Holly shouted after them.

Aunt Nicole had already booked flights to New Jersey.

Josh and Mom bumped along the winding dirt driveway. As they got farther from the house, Josh's thoughts turned to Dad. They'd already seen each other when Josh was in the hospital. Dad didn't have to report to jail until next month. But he'd still needed special permission to get on a plane and come to be with Josh and Mom.

Dad had stayed in Josh's room at the hospital, sleeping in a chair. Josh felt weird at first, as if Dad was a stranger. But pretty quick he realized Dad was still . . . *Dad*. Smiling and strong. Making the hospital staff laugh. Cheering Josh on as he slowly got better. He and Mom seemed okay, too. Together.

But there was a new sadness in Dad's eyes.

He'd tried to explain what had happened at the bank. He hadn't stolen millions of dollars, not exactly. It wasn't like he'd taken a bunch of money and spent it on himself. He and his boss had taken money from one of the bank's businesses and used it for another. Or something like that. It was complicated. It was illegal, and that was that.

"I knew I was breaking rules," Dad had said. "But I told myself I was helping the bank. And I figured nobody would get hurt."

He'd looked at Josh, tears in his eyes. "I sure was wrong," he said. "I'm so sorry, buddy."

Dad had lost his job, of course. Their house was for sale — they needed the money to pay Dad's lawyer bills. Mom would look for a job. Dad's jail was in New York, not too far away. And it wasn't too terrible. It was mostly for men who'd committed crimes at their jobs. Josh and Mom would be allowed to visit on Saturdays.

Josh looked out the window. They had turned out of Holly's driveway and onto the narrow country road. This latest fire had burned the forest on both sides of the street. Josh saw nothing but skeleton trees, reaching out with their sad, bony arms.

He thought about the animals who had lived here. Where had they gone? A lump grew in his throat as he imagined how they must feel. Maybe a little like he felt right now.

Lost.

CHAPTER 19

"Doing okay, sweetie?" Mom asked, taking his hand.

Josh slid his hand away and managed to nod. *Don't cry*, he told himself. He knew if he started crying it would be hard to stop.

"Why don't you open Holly's present?" Mom said.

Josh took a deep breath, then turned and lifted the box from the back seat. He'd figured it was a nature book or something. But the box was very light. He untied the ribbon, took off the lid, and stared in shock at the long, dried-out . . . *thing* . . . lying on a bed of tissue.

"Is that a dirty sock?" Mom asked, glancing over but quickly turning her focus back to the road.

"It's King's snake skin," Josh said with a little laugh. He shook his head as he pictured his cousin putting it in this box, tying it with a bow. Only Holly would give him such a . . . *different* kind of present.

"Oh my," Mom said, making a face.

Josh put the lid back on and set the box on the floor. He'd figure out some nice way to give it back to Holly when she came for Thanksgiving.

But as they drove slowly along that endless road, Josh thought of how hard it had been for King Kong to shed that skin. He pictured King's new skin, green and gold and glistening.

And it slowly came to Josh, why Holly had given him the present. What it meant. He thought back to the morning of the fire, when Holly had found him sitting alone in the woods. She'd told him about losing her dad, and how much she'd hated having to move. How tough it had been to start over. She'd said it was like shedding her skin.

And now Josh would have to shed his.

Maybe he and Holly weren't so different after all.

Josh sat for a while longer, thinking. And then Mom's purse started to buzz.

"Your phone!" Mom said. "I forgot I charged it for you. We must have service now."

Josh fished his phone out — it was going crazy with texts!

From Greg.

From Dad.

From his coach and the guys on his team.

When are you coming back?

We miss you!

Get well!

Josh's heart rose up. He answered Greg first.

Coming home tonight!

Then Dad.

Can't wait to see you.

Josh sent a few more texts and put his phone

into his pocket. He picked up the shoebox and opened it again. He looked at the snake skin and smiled to himself.

Greg was going to *freak* when he saw it! And Dad would think it was pretty cool, too, especially after Josh explained why Holly had given it to him.

Josh put the snake skin away and grabbed a muffin, then a brownie, then a cookie. He looked out the window, more intently now. They weren't out of the fire area yet. The forest was still burned. But for the first time, Josh noticed that there were some trees still standing. Strong trees that had somehow made it through the fire.

He put his hand on Mom's and looked at the long and curving road ahead. He leaned back in his seat.

They still had a ways to go, he knew. But they'd make it.

KEEP READING!

Turn the page to learn why Lauren
wrote this book and more facts about
wildfires.

WRITING ABOUT THE CALIFORNIA WILDFIRES

Dear Readers,

In many ways, the story of this I Survived book began in November 2018, when I received an email from a woman named Holly Fisher.

"You might have heard about the fire that has devastated my town of Paradise, California," she wrote.

My heart clenched as I read those words, because of course I had heard about Paradise. Just days before, on November 8, 2018, that bustling town of 28,000 people had been almost entirely destroyed by a fast-moving wildfire.

The Fisher family (from left): Josh, Sienna, Holly, and Lucas Fisher.

Holly went on to explain that her son, Lucas, and his friends read my books, and they wanted to share their experiences of the wildfire with me. "Maybe you should come here for a visit," Holly wrote.

I live in Connecticut, around three thousand miles from Paradise. But a few months later, I flew to California with my husband, David, and three of our four children. We drove past almond orchards and into the rolling foothills of the Sierra mountains, where Paradise sits high on a ridge. We met up with Holly and her husband, Josh, a firefighter who had helped save many lives when the fire raged through the town.

Holly and Josh took us on a drive through what was left of Paradise, and recounted their own stories from that terrifying day. They described their first glimpses of the fire, the thick column of smoke that appeared in the distance. They described how the air filled with glowing embers that were carried by the wind, and how quickly the bright morning turned midnight black from the smoke. Holly escaped by car with Lucas and his little sister, Sienna. Josh remained in Paradise with his fellow firefighters. He helped save hundreds of people who were trapped by the flames.

As we all rode together through the town, my family and I stared out the window in shock. On street after street after street, there was nothing but ruins. Houses had burned to the ground, with nothing left behind but twisted metal and fireplace bricks. Cars were destroyed, their bodies blackened, windows shattered, tires melted away. The thick forests were filled with skeleton trees.

The silence was eerie. We saw not one other living soul. Some houses had survived the fire, including the Fishers'. But months later, people still couldn't live in the town. There was no

The skeletons of cars and trucks after the fires in Paradise.

electricity. The water system had been poisoned by chemicals. The ground was covered with toxic ash that also made the air dangerous to breathe.

The next day, I met Paradise kids and teachers in their temporary schools. I got to spend time with Paradise Elementary principal Renee Henderson, and see how she and teachers were working nonstop to support their students and their families. I met Annie Finney, Lucas's teacher, who had turned her living room into a classroom until a temporary school could be found.

Three months later, David and I made a second visit to Paradise to check in with the Fishers and another family I had connected with — Greg and Nicole Weddig, and their daughter, Eleanor. Paradise was no longer silent. The air was filled with the sounds of chain saws and bulldozers. Much of the burned wreckage had been cleared away, and some new homes were beginning to go up. The Fishers were planning to move back into their house by Christmas. Both they and the Weddigs were hopeful, and doing whatever they could to keep their community together.

My time in Paradise showed me how destructive a wildfire can be. But I also saw how people can come together after a calamity, how they help one another, how they can move forward

The Weddig family (from left): Nicole, Eleanor, and Greg.

with their lives. This inspires me more than I can express. It was this feeling of hope and strength that I most wanted to capture in this I Survived book.

I wrote the book because many of the kids I met in Paradise asked me to write about wildfires. It's a work of historical fiction, like all the books in my series. That means that while all the facts are true, the town and the characters are fictional.

But as you probably already figured out, the characters are all named for members of the Fisher and Weddig family. This book is a tribute to them and to the many other people from Paradise — kids, parents, teachers — I feel lucky to know.

Lauren Tarshis

MORE FACTS

As always, I learned so much researching this book, and couldn't fit it all into the story. So here is some additional information about wildfires and giant reptiles, and other facts I wanted to share:

WILDFIRES REALLY ARE GETTING MORE DESTRUCTIVE

Wildfires have always been part of nature. But since the 1980s, wildfires in California and other parts of the world have been getting bigger and more destructive. Fifteen of the twenty most destructive fires in California history have all happened since the year 2000.

Why is this?

Scientists agree that climate change is a main cause of these bigger and more destructive wildfires. Like many parts of the world, California is hotter and drier than it used to be. Hotter and drier air means forests get parched — there's less moisture in the soil and plants. This means that fires start more easily, and burn faster.

But another cause of today's wildfire crisis is that for more than one hundred years, we've been trying to put out every wildfire we can. Now scientists and experts understand that this policy was not wise. Small wildfires (and even some larger fires) are a natural part of the life of a forest. They burn away dead and diseased trees. Without these natural fires, a forest becomes overgrown, with more to burn once a wildfire starts.

THE 2018 FIRE SEASON WAS THE MOST DESTRUCTIVE IN CALIFORNIA HISTORY

California has thousands of wildfires in a typical year. Most are small and are put out quickly. What was different about 2018 was not simply that there was an especially large number of fires — about 8,000. It was that three of those fires were "megafires," highly destructive fires that burned more than 100,000 acres.

A hillside erupts in flames during the Mendocino Complex Fire.

The largest was the Mendocino Complex Fire, which burned 459,000 acres. The Carr

Fire, which is the one mentioned in this book, burned 230,000 acres and destroyed 1,604 houses and buildings. The Camp Fire, which destroyed Paradise, burned 153,000 acres and was also the deadliest fire in California in fifty years — eighty-five people were killed.

In total, wildfires in California burned 1.8 million acres in 2018. That's bigger than the state of Delaware.

Wildfires don't only happen in California, though. They can happen anywhere there are trees and grass to burn.

California has had the most wildfires of any state in recent years, followed by Nevada and Oregon. I was surprised that Oklahoma was number four. In 2017, a megafire raged across the grassy land of Oklahoma and northern Texas, burning 781,000 acres.

And wildfires are a problem all across the world. In 2019, millions of acres in Australia burned in the country's worst fires in nearly a century.

THE BIGGEST WILDFIRE IN US HISTORY HAPPENED IN 1910

The Great Fire of 1910, also called the Big Burn, was the biggest wildfire in American history. It destroyed three million acres, mostly in Montana and Northern Idaho. Eighty-seven people died, mostly firefighters.

The Big Burn is fascinating to learn about. If you do some research on your own, you'll see that it changed history. It was that fire that caused US

A crew works to fight a fire, circa 1910.

leaders to decide to fight all wildfires, no matter what (which, as you now know, was not a great idea).

Also, everyone should know about the fire-fighter Ed Pulaski. He helped save dozens of

Every wildland firefighter carries a Pulaski in their kit.

firefighters who were trapped in the flames by leading them into an old mine. He also invented a firefighting tool that is still used today — called the Pulaski. It's a simple tool. One side is a small hoe that can also work as a shovel to move dirt. The other is an ax for cutting brush, limbs, and small trees. Wildland firefighters use it for making fire lines, clearing away brush, and digging up "hot potatoes," underground roots that could reignite a wildfire that's been put out.

WHAT CAN BE DONE TO PREVENT WILDFIRES?

We can all help prevent wildfires by being careful when we are in wild places. But experts say that

Firefighters do a controlled burn to protect houses from the Ranch Fire in August 2018.

the most important step we can take is to allow some kinds of wildfires to burn. In California and across the West, firefighters are using what are known as "controlled burns" to thin out forests. They set these fires at special times, when winds are low and the weather isn't too hot and dry. They let the fires burn through a small portion of a forest, to remove dead and sick trees and brush. They work carefully to make sure the fires don't spread.

There are also steps that people in fire-prone areas can take around their homes. Many are removing trees and bushes and grasses that can catch fire. They're replacing them with plants that don't burn and can stop fires from spreading, like ice plants and aloe.

HERE'S WHAT YOU CAN DO ABOUT WILDFIRES

- If you are camping, only make a campfire where it is permitted. Make sure your parents and helpers put out all fires before you leave.
- Talk about wildfires with your family. If you live in a fire-prone area, make a family plan. Invite a firefighter to your class to talk about how you can stay safe.
- If you see even a small fire in the wild, get away quickly and tell an adult. Remember that a small fire can become a huge fire in minutes.

And one last thing . . .

NEVER BUY A BIG REPTILE AS A PET

I loved creating the characters of Bubbles and King Kong. The most important thing I learned is that these magnificent animals should not be kept as pets.

Large reptiles animals are hard to care for, which is why so many are abandoned in the wild. Most of these creatures don't survive. But in some parts of the country they not only survive — they thrive. And this has caused some big problems.

In Florida, for instance, there are an estimated two hundred thousand Burmese pythons on the loose in the Everglades, basically devouring everything in sight — bird eggs, other reptiles, rabbits, foxes, even deer. Some animals have vanished from the Everglades entirely because of the pythons' presence.

If you love reptiles, show your love by learning all you can about them and letting them live in the wild, where they belong.

Biologists hold a 15-foot Burmese python found in the Everglades in Florida.

WILDFIRE VEHICLES AND GEAR

Here's a look at some of the special gear and vehicles made just for wildfires.

AIR TANKER

Air tankers can drop up to 20,000 gallons of water or fire retardant in one flight. This DC-10 air tanker is dropping fire retardant near Santa Barbara, California.

HUEY HELICOPTER

Cal Fire buys used helicopters from the military and makes changes to them so they can fight fires. Bell UH-1H Super Hueys are used to move firefighters, for water drops, and sometimes for rescue missions.

BRUSH TRUCK

Brush trucks, also called wildland engines, are smaller than regular fire trucks. They have four-wheel drive so they can drive over rough ground to the site of a fire. Unlike regular fire trucks, which have to stop before they can pump water from their hose, brush trucks can pump water while moving. This feature is called "pump and roll." It allows firefighters to attack the edge of a large fire quickly and stop the spread of flames..

PACK

Wildland firefighters can often be out on the fire line for days or weeks at a time. Their packs include special pockets for water bottles; fuel containers; and small items like headlamps, batteries, GPS trackers, weather trackers, first aid kits, and glow sticks. Firefighters can attach tools like folding saws and pocketknives to them as well. There is also a special pocket where they can quickly grab and deploy their fire shelters. The packs sit low on their backs so that firefighters' bodies remain balanced while cutting and sawing and moving through brushy terrain.

FIRE SHELTER

Fire shelters look like fireproof sleeping bags. They are used as a last resort when a firefighter is caught in the middle of a fire. The shelters come packed in shoebox-sized cases. When firefighters need to use them, they pull a cord and shake out the folded shelters. The firefighter climbs in and protects their nose, mouth, and face by keeping close to the ground. Fire shelters can withstand heat up to 800 degrees and keep a firefighter safe for a few minutes while flames pass overhead.

SELECTED BIBLIOGRAPHY

The Big Burn: Teddy Roosevelt and the Fire that Saved America, by Timothy Egan, New York, NY, Houghton Mifflin Harcourt, 2009

Burning Planet: The Story of Fire Through Time, by Andrew C. Scott, Oxford, UK, Oxford University Press, 2018

"California Burning," by William Finnegan, *The New York Review of Books,* August 16, 2018

"California Knew the Carr Fire Could Happen. It Failed to Prevent It," by Keith Schneider, ProPublica, December 18, 2018

"Destined to Burn," by writers of the *Sacramento Bee,* April 2019

"Fire on the Mountain," by Brian Mockenhaupt, *The Atlantic,* June 2014

Firestorm: How Wildfire Will Shape Our Future, by Edward Struzik, Washington, DC, Island Press, 2017

Megafire: The Race to Extinguish a Deadly Epidemic of Flame, by Michael Kodas, New York, NY, Houghton Mifflin Harcourt, 2017

Wildfire: On the Front Lines with Station 8, by Heather Hansen, Seattle, WA, Mountaineers Books, 2018

Other I Survived books about fires:

THE AUTHOR IN FRONT OF A FIRE TRUCK IN PARADISE, CALIFORNIA, WITH FIREFIGHTER JOSH FISHER.

Lauren Tarshis's *New York Times* bestselling I Survived series tells the stories of young people and their resilience and strength in the midst of unimaginable disasters and times of turmoil. Lauren has brought her signature warmth, integrity, and exhaustive research to topics such as the September 11 attacks, the American Revolution, Hurricane Katrina, the Battle of D-Day, and other events that shaped history and our lives today. Lauren lives in Connecticut with her family, and can be found online at laurentarshis.com.